A Phoenix Still Rising

By

Mary Farrell

ISBN: 978-1-915819-20-8

dedicated to Steve and Nikki Cawte

for being who you are

for doing what you do

OTHER TITLES BY IMPSPIRED

Layers of Rust –
by Micaela Melnic

Addicted to Dog Magazines -
by Laura Stamp

Spun Yarns and Woven Words –
by North Coast Writers

daddy's girl -
by Isabelle Cory

Perdition Falls –
by Will Storrs

The Alchemy of Then –
by Jim Bates

Tobias: and the Isle of Justice –
by Mark Pearce

INTRODUCTION

A Phoenix Still Rising is the final book in the Trilogy which records Mary Farrell's journey of self-challenge in the world of Creative Writing, the first two books being *It's like Walking a Tightrope* and *Out of the Chrysalis.* Over the last three years, she has tried to hone her skills by writing in many varied genres, using many different techniques. Sometimes her attempts ended in ashes, but like the Phoenix, she is determined to continue to rise. The fact that this is the last book in this Grail-Quest Trilogy is not by any means a reflection of complacency that she thinks she has done all she needs. It merely underlines the fact she realises she must now concentrate her efforts with the same determination on her Trilogy of short stories, The Circle. Steadier on that Tightrope, further out of the Chrysalis and continuing to rise like a Phoenix, she intends to persist with tenacity in her journey to advance and improve.

ACKNOWLEDGEMENTS

The Creative Writing world is a generous and supportive one, right across the globe.
In Northern Ireland, the members of the Writing Groups which I facilitate - North Coast Writers, Words Inc and Sanderlings - have all been encouraging and energizing with their feedback and creative advice. It is a pleasure indeed to work with them.
Over the last three years while writing this Trilogy, I have also been made a very welcome member of the Portrush Writers Group, led by Kate Murphy, and This Writing Thing, a Writing Group in the North-West led by Sue Divin. Many grateful thanks also to Kathleen McCracken and Frankie Sewell of Ulster University in Coleraine for their generosity in inviting me to attend their Creative Writing Lectures.
When it came to the many Writing Courses I had the privilege of attending, there are far too many inspirational teachers out there to name individually. From my heart, I am deeply grateful that you all have been so open-handed with your expertise, patient with your explanations and altruistic with your advice. I will however always be grateful to Bernie McGill in particular for guiding my first shaky steps along the path to look for my Creative Voice.
The increasing support I am receiving from overseas is both humbling and invigorating. What a joy it is to be included in such a universal community. Thank you deeply.

I am very grateful indeed to Maureen Hamilton for the time she spent, and her attention to detail, when she was editing all three of these Collections. Her tightening and polishing skills are deeply appreciated, as is her friendship.

Without Steve Cawte, the Editor of Impspired Press, these Collections would literally not exist. His support, advice and editing expertise – quite apart from his continual good humour and endless patience – have made the whole process of publishing this Trilogy an easier and more pleasurable experience than I could ever have dreamt.

Causeway u3a - both the Committee and many of its general body of members - have been incredibly generous with their support, both personal and practical, and with technical help for the launching of my books. I am deeply grateful to Barbara Foster and Brendan Mullan, the current Chairperson and Treasurer. Here also I would like to thank the Royal Court Hotel, Portrush, for making Book Launches such an enjoyable experience for everyone.

Lastly, as always, I would like to thank my four grandsons, Alexander, Taylor, Charlie and Jamie for the love, hugs and laughter with which they continue to light up my life.

Literary Acknowledgements:

Hearth Matters appeared in the Anthology *Love, Loss and Cardiac Issues* published by Impspired Press, 2022.

Just stop…think, Kintsukuroi unmastered, Magpie left, and *Breached* appeared in *Spun Yarns and Woven Words,* the second Anthology by North Coast Writers, published by Impspired Press, 2023.

Ghosts and *Secrets and Lies* were performed on the Tenx9 stage in Northern Ireland in 2022. *The Journey* was performed in 2023 for Tenx9 as part of The Steinbeck Festival in Limavady, Northern Ireland.

CONTENTS

Kintsukuroi unmastered

~ the art of fixing broken pottery, usually with gold ~

She'd really tried, she had! *I never loved her…only you,* he'd bleated, finally realising she was going to leave him. And it was probably true, she'd thought ruefully. But a realization which covered too little, came too late. She'd tried… but despite the white heat of first couplings, the molten gold of her compassion, the blood-shot embers of their clinkered love, she couldn't make it work, not even for the twins' sake. Cases in the boot, the children with her parents, her rings obsolete on his bedside table, she drove away without a backward glance.

hearth matters

the Cottage snivelled

as it remembered

there had been trilling laughs and dancing feet, the swirls and curls of toddlers tumbling

smells of yeast and crusts, savouries and sweet crumbles, beer a-hopping and mint-sharp teas

just-birthed lambs, crook-eared sheepdogs, ancient cats curled tight on hearthstones

with love flowing tween souls sealed by kiss-warm hugs, sweet caresses and tight holdings

the Cottage wept deep sobs

as it remembered

there had been such pain with the fire, as beams broke wide and rafters crashed

furniture withered, flame veined curtains, lino globbed in tiny pustules

photos blacked out of memory, precious carvings dissolved, keepsakes melted

and the next days dawn crept low over skeleton walls, charred ruins and the sharp taste of ash

the Cottage healed slowly

as it remembered

after the clearance the first smudge of green in the grave-brown earth, grassroots regrown

birds quested worms in the trenches upturned and micelings sniffed and snuffled for seeds

lichen smoothed green the stumps of foundations, moss ironed out cracks in walls heat-blown

and the next Spring brought colour and cubs, fur babies and new birthed, all in Natures rebound

and life thrived and continued, continued and thrived

as life always must

Magpie left

She'd left him. Why?

He hadn't seen it coming. He'd fashioned a nest of her favourite colours, textures, sensations. The flat was redecorated, IKEA raided for sprigs and baubles, cushions and bedding, all to her liking. Gluten-free packets in the cupboards, organic veg in the fridge. He'd swollen large with her delight when they'd bought the disco ball together, giddy with laughter at its tackiness. She'd giggled and swayed and shimmied that night, with silver lights dancing off her blue-black hair. He'd thought they'd mated for life. On Solstice Eve, he came home from work, his arms full of sunflowers, and found her note.

I have to go. Goodbye.

Time stopped as the Earth jolted, then resurged but with such a slow crawl. The Longest Day became the longest day. For months, years afterwards, he haunted her familiar lairs, hovering low with a heavyweight heart.

She was gone.

He was alone.

Breached

~ *(s)He came in through the bathroom window,* the Beatles, 1969 ~

The Colonel watched him on the security monitor, sidling along the wall, ducking behind bushes, assuming he was invisible. Slender body, black-clad, sinister balaclava, silent sneakers. He edged ever closer to the house until he disappeared from view below the CCTV camera beside the window of a second-floor bathroom. The Colonel, straight-backed, lifted a revolver from a dresser drawer in his bedroom, and with a firm step went to wait beside the bathroom door, the only exit from that particular bathroom. The others were all ensuite.

And then he waited. He knew well how to stand motionless, had done so in many battle zones throughout his career. As he counted away the seconds, then the minutes, waiting for the burglar to ease open the door, he grew calmer and more resolute. No-one was going to invade his home, breach his defences.

The handle began to drop by millimetres, making no sound. A door gap widened in just the same way and a tiny silhouette slithered through onto the landing. The Colonel, behind a large palm plant, allowed the figure to take three paces away from him before barking out, *Stop right there or I'll shoot.* Even he was surprised at how much satisfaction he received from the theatricality of the phrase.

The figure stopped. It only took seconds for all poise and grace to melt away, the shoulders to slump and the torso to curve as if in reaction to a solar plexus punch. The Colonel, flooding with the first surging of adrenaline, was disconcerted. What to do now? Frogmarch the villain down to the hallway and phone the Police? But first things first. *Take off that mask and turn around!*

And that's when everything changed.

As a trembling hand pulled off the balaclava, a black ponytail uncoiled. A blanched face, oval eyes brimming with tears, looked up at him, lower lip trembling. She tried to speak but could only stammer *Ple…ple…please.* Disconcerted before, the Colonel was now thrown totally off-guard. He had been prepared to stare down a thug, intent on robbery, but found it difficult to keep waving a gun at this tiny slip of a girl, who was obviously terrified. *Walk in front of me, down the stairs to the hall, and mind, no funny business!* Somehow this time, the crime drama scripting failed to ring true. He just felt uncomfortable, as if he was bullying a child who needed help.

Once in the hall, with the gun he motioned her to a chair beside the telephone table. Of course, he had a mobile, it *was* the twenty-first century! but he'd always been reluctant to dispense with the landline in the hallway. *Before I call the Police, give me your story so that I know what to say to them.* That came out all wrong, he realized immediately. He should be calling the Police first. What did it matter what her story was? Why was he even asking? Perhaps it was the surprise of finding a *She* when he'd expected a *He.*

In a child's voice, little above a whisper, a tale was told. Of an invalid mother, a father long since rotting in his grave, and of her only sibling, an elder brother, just four months out of Pentonville, back home to threaten and bully. He studied Council Tax Data to register any pensioners who lived alone. He had a mate in the Town Hall, see, who had access to such restricted information. Then he'd case houses in the Riverside area of the City. She was just seventeen but instead of studying at school last term for her A-levels, he'd taught her to open locks, tricks to improve night vision, how to swivel through small spaces and tread lightly. *He'd* put on too much weight during that last stretch inside. He said she'd have to do it for him from now on, or else Mum……..! And that line was never finished. Her imagination created worse terrors than his words ever could. This was her fourth time breaking in somewhere, and she was so so sorry but what else could she do! She was scared of him, but her Mum was terrified.

As he listened, the gun dropped lower and lower. Adrenaline leached away, and by the time the young voice faded out, he too felt slumped. This poor child was no dangerous intruder, no threat to him. What was to be done?

Later that night . . .

The last Police Car had left. The kitchen sink was full of empty cups. The air was still quivering from sharp-shot questions, hesitant answers, accusations, affirmations, promises and at last, finally, now the hint of returning peace. A second tale had been told, this time mostly fictional. Of a couple meeting randomly on a park bench and of a nerve-taut teenager unexpectedly breaking down at the kindness of an offered sandwich. The same family background had been described truthfully, but the rest of *this* tale had been devised by the ex-Military man who all his life had fought against the abuse of power. It had not been disclosed that a different burglary of his house had been planned by the Colonel himself and the young girl, secreting compromising evidence to incriminate her brother. Suggestions had however been made to the Police to check here, here and of course there…and don't forget the name of his accomplice in the Town Hall!

The Colonel sat on the same chair in the hall where the first tale had been disclosed. He was exhausted but had one more task to do that long long night. An Uber had been dispatched to fetch Mum. He was waiting to welcome her to stay for a while at his home while her daughter was being questioned, and her situation assessed. Then they could both stay until her son was charged. His lawyer has reassured them that, considering the circumstances and the level of duress employed, any charges for the first three burglaries would be severely mitigated if the Colonel would stand up for such an under-age defendant. Of course he would, without question.

As he waited he mused. It was twenty years ago today. Twenty years since Edith had died. Twenty years in a nowhere land without a wife or children. They'd never been blest with a family. But strangely he felt blest now. His barricades had been smashed, and his future held more such invasions, but for the first time in years, he looked forward to waking up tomorrow.

Footnote:- *Written in response to Paul McCartney's Set at Glastonbury Festival, 25th June 2022. There are five words, phrases or lines from Beatle lyrics in the piece.*

Soul-mated

A new recruit to Tinder, he was spell-bound, enchanted. Her photos on the dating profile revealed someone, like him, with a deep commitment to Goth Culture. Dark-rimmed eyes, various nose and ear piercings, black outfits of many fabrics layered like cobwebs. The vibe from her messages however was very different. A girlish tone soothed and flirted, teased and complimented him.

Incredible they had so much in common. Black Sabbath their favourite group, they both owned an ebony cat called Midnight. Top of their *To Do* list for many years now had been a pilgrimage to Whitby for the Goth Weekend. Could they perhaps go together when it was next held? They'd matched in the third week in October, had messaged often every day since. It was unfortunate that she lived in a 'Dark Spot' wi-fi area. Video calls were therefore out of the question. Still, they didn't have too long to wait until they met in person, only ten days until the first Sunday night they were both off work and could meet up for dinner. Equidistant from them both was The Black Swan Inn, whose dining room had earned four stars on TripAdvisor. He'd checked it out with due diligence, he so wanted her to dine well at their first meeting.

With the venue settled, she suggested parking in the nearby cemetery Carpark, and meeting him under the

Lych Gate at the entrance to the nearby Church. How romantic he thought! The walls of The Black Swan were lined with photos of newlyweds taken under the thatch of that beautiful Tudor gateway into the Church grounds.

As he drove to the rendezvous he practised lines, compliments, interesting stories, all designed to impress. He was early, of course he was! So stressed by the time her tiny car turned into the carpark, he'd swear he could hear the blood pumping in his veins. She was all he'd imagined.... and more! After he stammered a few stop and start sentences, he calmed enough to tune in to what she was saying. Her grandmother was buried in that cemetery, could they pay a quick visit? They *had* a few minutes before their 8.00 pm dinner reservation, hadn't they?

As he followed her on the curved path to the left between the stones, he mused at how dark it was, but then remembered. Of course, the clocks always went back this weekend. As she was passing under a high curving yew tree with heavy earth-bound branches, she turned, grabbed him around the waist, and moved in close. The embrace he had dreamt of on so many of his recent sleepless nights. The kiss went on and on and on... until at last, when they were both breathless, she nuzzled into his neck with a mewling satisfied sigh. It was a long long time afterward before he realised that he now had two permanent tiny red marks on his neck. After all, he could never see himself in a mirror ever again.

Subsumed ... Resumed

she walked down the aisle, her fairy-tale come true

until the honeymoon magic began to dissipate

be reasonable, I have to travel for work

she grew used to being alone

under his thumb, her sister hissed

my schedule's just so busy, babes

every hidden receipt told a different story

do you really think I'm so gullible, she fumed

registered Bank Account in your name only, Ma'am

each day millimetres of self-esteem crawling back

she told her sister she intended to leave him

until I've the escape all sorted, say nothing

my own flat key, and it's mine, just mine

every damning document to the solicitor

divorced at last! My new life begins.

Ghosts

This piece was performed on stage on October 28th, 2022, at a Tenx9 event in Flowerfield Arts Centre in Portstewart, Northern Ireland. All stories told at Tenx9 must be autobiographical. The designated theme was 'Ghosts'.

As a storyteller, Charles Dickens had it nailed! with the Ghosts of Christmas Past, Present and Future. Well, let's not spoil the mood of the evening by considering any Present or Future figures in the current political climate. Let's just concentrate on the Ghosts of the Past. Now, I don't mean spectres or ghouls or any unsavoury beasties. I'm thinking more of various Sliding Doors scenarios, as in the film. What alternative pasts might I have had if I'd made different choices, taken different pathways? Are those other Me s out there in the ether, haunting, ghost-like, in some kind of Einstein-ian parallel universe??? So, with you all as wingmen, let us risk a trip down my alternative Memory Lane.

The first major intriguing choice I had was which University to go to after receiving my A Level results. Queens, Trinity, Bristol, Manchester or wait for it … I'd already been offered a place by my delightfully nepotistic aunt, the then Dean, at Loyola Marymount University in Los Angeles. And I chose…Queens! Looking back at that particular closed Sliding Door, everything in me screeches ...*were you insane!?!* Hollywood, Rodeo Drive, Graumans Chinese Theatre, Santa Monica, even Disneyland...and in 1971, at the height of the Troubles, I chose the Falls, Sandy Row, checkpoints, handbags searches and bomb scares. Now I'd had been highly programmed throughout my teens in the usual Norn Iron religious way to believe that living anywhere outside the Province would lead to a life of sin, debauchery, and eternal damnation. You'd think, screams my present self, those visions of my potential future downfall would be actual attractive inducements to flee these shores. Again, I screech *Was I insane?*

But let's look at the particular Ghost who might be standing in front of you here tonight had I made an alternative choice then. **(Indicate the space to my right).** Meet Mary Stowkoski - Farrell, thrice divorced with a larger financial settlement each time, skin like brown leather from a life spent on Golf Courses and Pacific Beaches. A pleasant little bungalow in Long Beach near the Queen Mary, an apartment in Lake Tahoe for winter skiing trips. A chequered past of festivals, Beat Poets and possibly a little too much knowledge garnered over the years about the effects of marijuana, and the nocturnal habits of male surfers. Like Blanche in the television show 'Golden Girls ', she now has carved out a pleasant life around shopping malls, Whist afternoons, beauty Parlours, not to mention the Seniors Speed Dating night every month at the Shamrock Club, a hostelry almost exclusively peopled with those of the Irish Diaspora.

Let me look at you Mary Stowkoski - Farrell, and for the nth time, I sob… *I turned down California???*

Let's move on to another Sliding Door. What career did I choose? because dependant on that, was the issue of where I'd live for most of my adult life. After gaining a degree from Queens, in the same year, I was offered both a place on a Teacher Training Course and an engagement ring from a Northern Ireland native. And so that Sliding Door Underground Train led to 26 years teaching in Ballymoney, and a home bought in Portrush. Not a disaster in so many many ways! I'd inherited my father's teaching genes and faced the work and the pupils with enthusiasm. And until a very amicable divorce 19 years ago, a compatible marriage saw the birth and growth of two children. However, as we waved goodbye to them when they left home, we also packed our bags and waved cheerily to each other as we too moved out. All four of us had grown up in different directions. And the different direction for me was to France, following my souls call, as irresistible a Siren need for me as breathing. But what if instead of becoming a teacher in Ballymoney, I'd become one in Boulogne or Biarritz. What if instead of living in Portrush, I'd lived my life in Paris or Perpignan.

So, let's meet another alternative Ghost. Bonsoir to Marie Farrelle. **(Indicate the space to my right).**

Impeccably dressed, she's half my girth, the result of many years smoking endless Gauloise. She speaks with her hands (no difference there then!), drinks at least ten cups of strong black coffee a day, and considers any casserole cooked without at least two cloves of garlic to be an under-nourished one. She controls her pupils with a straight back and steely glare, brooking no nonsense. The family have a small cottage in Andalusia where they spend the summers. Her two children are thus tri-lingual, speaking fluent French, Spanish and English with the faintest hint of an Irish brogue as they spend a fortnight with her Irish family every October mid-term. Ah Marie, the *Fraternité* I feel with your Ghost, or should that be *Sororité,* my sister. Anyway, take a seat over there with Mary Stowkoski-Farrell. Like Scrooge on Christmas Eve, we've one last Ghost to meet.

My last Sliding Door refers to the choice of pastime I took up when I returned from France to live in Northern Ireland five years ago, needing to begin a new life. I chose to sign up for the Creative Writing Course, then run by Bernie McGill in this very Flowerfield Arts Centre. Hedging my bets, I also signed up for the u3a Beginners Bridge, as a Friend of the Riverside Theatre and as a volunteer in a Charity Shop. Now it has been hinted to me throughout my life that I'm a tad of a full-on type. Don't see it myself, but hey, whatever. But what if I hadn't gone hammer and tongs into the world of Creative Writing. Well, I wouldn't be at this podium talking to you now, that's for sure. What if that Door had slid shut five years ago with me on the other side of it, along with the Bridge, Theatre and Charity Shop work.

So let me introduce you to the final Ghost of the evening. **(Indicate right again).** Her name is Katerina Farrelli. As her dramatic flair, nourished by her new theatrical friends began to burn more brightly, she stopped using her original Christian name and changed to her second one. That was meant to be Catherine, but her Baptismal Priest had a strong devotion to Latin, and as the Holy Water flowed into the font, Catherine flowed into Katerina. The feeling then grew in her that her surname could also do with a bit of jazzing-up, so she became Katerina Farrelli by Deed Poll three years ago.

Not only did her name become more flamboyant, but so did her attire. Seizing the opportunity in the Charity Shop to be the first to rifle through the incoming bags, she had the pick of the proffered wardrobes. A problem? – how to wear designer clothes (you'd be amazed at how many pass through the Charity shops) but also to create a Bohemian style which would make her stand out in her new Am-Dram world. And of course, she needed outfits for a respectable 'alter ego' at the twice weekly Bridge meets. Katerina, **(indicate right again)** has had to draw up a strict wardrobe schedule for her three personas. Not quite twinset and fake pearls for the Bridge Club but close. Dungarees for trawling through the bags delivered to the Charity Shop. And the vital third wardrobe as you can see, from the bandana, handwoven serape and harem trousers, to fit in with her new Thespian Circle.

So now you've met my three ghostly alternatives, seen what I might have become in other circumstances. As other storytellers here tonight will no doubt ask in their performances, *who you gonna call?* Me? these alternative-life ghosts??? I think not! A Tenx9 podium is scary enough for me right now. So, I'll just leave you with this thought...*don't look behind you!?!*

The Island

Every evening when the last ferry sailed, filled with sun-fried or wind-swept or rain-sodden day trippers, the hikers and bikers, harassed parents of toddlers and teenagers fidgety from Xbox withdrawal, the island would fold back in on itself. In summer, a descending sun sealed the harbour mouth with bands of orange, vermilion, and deep deep rose. In winter, heavy clouds dropped from a higher arc and settled in hovering mode on the crests of the sloping hills. In a ritual he chose never to break, he would stand on the quay in all weathers to watch the last ferry leave.

As it passed the buoys marking the midway point from the mainland, the Islanders too settled into themselves. Their bodies would expand in the returned peace, freed from a freeze of polite smiles and the bread-and-butter pressure to say *can I help you* to tourists. Tides would creep up beaches, sweeping them clean of the day's debris - footprints, cigarette butts, dropped coins or earrings. Even the gulls, voraciously intrusive in daytime, with the fading light would settle to roost behind sheltering harbour walls. In the horseshoe bay, moored boats swayed or bobbed, waves slapped or caressed hulls and always, flags would tug at the tops of masts.

He would wake convincing himself today would be the day she would come, but each evening he stood at the shore, his hopes fading in the fragmented wake of the landward boat. Since she slammed the outside door for what he hadn't realised then would be the last time, he knew in his core that if she came to rest anywhere it would be back on the Island. She'd grown up there: the red fuchsia, the silver-shim waves, the sting of salt on her lips, all of that was in her DNA, her very pores. She *would* come back here in the end. She had to because he didn't know where else to look. He'd sold their city flat, moved sideways in the firm to a position in which he could work from home, rented a cottage on the Island. His desk squatted below the window overlooking the jetty, from where he could watch the ferry passengers disembark. And then he waited, throughout every long day.

She never came. He never left. A few Islanders, those to whom he'd told his story, still ensure there are always fresh flowers on his grave.

The Hawthorn Tree

the hawthorn tree drooped to

nuzzle the ground   strained to caress

the grass in a perfect circle   the lure of safe magic

beckoned below the canopy   the branches whispered

a multi stringed symphony of overlapping voices

those who had planted those who had protected

those who had come for sanctuary

behind the music a gentle harmony

of presences layered enchantment

we are here   they chorused

with a gentle flutter

of gossamer wings

and a

light

breeze

of

fairie

Murder They Wrote

(Written by Mary Farrell, this is the beginning of a Murder Mystery Story begun in January 2023, continued by the members of Words Inc, a Creative Writing Group run by Libraries NI, with a segment added each week by five different Group members)

Murder They Wrote
January 18th, 2023

Huntley Hall was not a place anyone would visit of their own free will. None of the family members would have returned to it on this dark November Friday evening if it had not been for the reading of Arthur Shrike's will tomorrow. At exactly noon the following day, all would be revealed by Mr. Thornton of Thornton, Thornton and Puddledike, the most prestigious law firm in the area for as long as anyone could remember. The tedious uncomfortable journey over bleak moorland roads had been unpleasant enough the first time to attend the austere Funeral Service and perfunctory Interment in the family crypt. To have to return within four weeks was too much to ask ... except for those driven by need or greed.

Arthur Shrike had adored this ugly Early Victorian building. He had insisted it was the true home of the dark Muse who inspired his gloomy haunted paintings which, by the end of his life, had been exchanging for six figure sums. His young bride had detested it. The children wiped its dust from their feet as soon as they came of age. Just after the departure of the last, the Wife, unable to stand living there any longer, threw herself to her death from its highest turret.

Mrs. Grimsden, the housekeeper, wore a tight smile as she carried through the drinks tray before dinner. Three of Mr. Shrike's children were gathered in the Drawing Room. The youngest son, John, had been sent to the jungles of the Amazon four years previously on a classified military mission. The Army had six months later declared him to be Missing in Action, but his siblings felt in their bones that he had died some horrible unspeakable death. Nonetheless, they did not mourn him.

Drinks were served to the three remaining heirs in the order of their precedence. The boys, by their father's decree, had all been named after English kings. Mr. Shrike was nothing if not patriotic. The eldest, Henry, had ordered a very large whisky, Charles a soda water. Lastly Mrs. Grimsden gave a very dry sherry to 'the poor girl'. She was always referred to as that. Coming last as she did after three lusty boys, the Wife was ordered to name her. Female children didn't matter to Arthur Shrike. She was called Marisa. All her childhood 'the poor girl' had been tormented by her three elder brothers; calling her names, placing frogs in her nursery desk, leaving her lost in the woods, soaking her with water when they played down by the lake. Mrs. Grimsden had always had a soft spot for the girl but could never show it. The boys would have noticed and made her life all the more unbearable because of it.

The segments which follow: Red Herrings … or not?

January 25th : Maura Doran

~ Significant points in Part Two ~
*The housekeeper Mrs Grimsden, who has a French mother, finds out that Marisa now living in Paris, is engaged to a leading French Art Collector.
* Marisa's bedroom overlooks the back of the house while the bedrooms of her two brothers overlook its front, with a view of a ha-ha and woods.
* Looking at the Friday evening dinner menu, the cook has a penchant for cooking highly spiced dishes.

February 1st : Ruth Holloway

~ Significant points in Part Three ~
* The third son John, MIA in the Amazon, returns home in time for the reading of the will. He is not mentioned in it as everyone thought he was dead.
* Marisa is left two horses, Charles and Henry receive one

million pounds each.
For some reason this is not enough for Charles who needs more.
* Huntley Hall is to be sold, with the proceeds given to a Charity chosen by Charles.
* No decision is clarified about the many priceless paintings in the Hall painted, and owned, by Arthur Shrike.

February 10th: Ian Garner

~ Significant points in Part Four ~
* Charles and his brother Henry have been plotting about the Will for some years. Finding out where their father had kept it, they knew its contents.
* They had also hired Investigators who had informed them that John was still alive, and updated them with what he had been doing all these years.
* On an afternoon walk in the woods after Saturday Lunch, Henry loses sight of Charles at the same time as he hears rifle shots close to him.

February 16th: Jenny Millar

~ Significant points in Part Five ~
**(Flashback to late Friday night)* Marisa confesses to the Housekeeper, Mrs Grimsden, that her mother did not commit suicide by jumping from the tower.
* She, Marisa, was present at the turret-top when her brother John pushed their mother to her death.
*Mrs Grimsden also has a long-kept secret of her own,

which will inevitably be revealed when Marisa tells all, as she intends to do after the reading of the will the next morning.

February 22nd: Kenny Campbell

~ Significant points in Part Six ~
*Charles is injured, but he and Henry make their way back to the Hall.
*The rifle was fired by Marisa's fiancé, Gabriel, with the intent to kill the brothers, leaving Marisa the sole heir.
*He and Marisa had planned this shooting together.

~ so what happened next? ~

A First of January Tale

Quill poised between his lean fingers, brow furrowed, Mr B Ignatius Wolf, BA (Drama), PhD (Forensic Science) scowled at the blank page in front of him. Not a disciple of self-restraint, he disapproved of the whole concept of Resolutions at any time of year. He chose to see this current exercise more in the light of a 'Note to Self' rather than drawing up commandments to restrict his future behaviour. Settling to his task, he began to write with a flourish, being fond of lavishness.

Point One:.

While it is necessary in these current times to be wary of excessive spending, I may have been a tad too parsimonious this festive season. In future, I shall seek out a better-quality dinner. No more old birds for me! The meat was stringy, the bones thin and marrowless, the giblets wizened. No amount of the black sausage, plump dumplings and thick Red Eye Gravy I enjoyed later in the second Course could compensate for those shortcomings. I must accept that I will need to focus on snaring younger birds in the future in order to sate my tastes.

Point Two:

I must adopt a regular self-care programme. Skillful hairstyling would help to disguise those horrible large ears I've inherited from Grandpa Lupin, and I really must do something about my teeth. I haven't been to the Dentist in years. Capping them maybe ... but certainly a descaling to remove that unpleasant yellowish tinge. As for waxing, well... my forearms and legs are long overdue.

Point Three:

I've been pondering over it for years but I really must come to some decision about moving. Those Woodcutters are completely overrunning this neck of the forest. There's far too many of them now. Here in search of work indeed! Have they no trees where they come from? I can hardly stroll down a single pathway without having to hide from lumber carts. And the noise! Shouting, trees crashing, sawing ... it's all too much. I'll have to find somewhere else altogether, where I can go quietly about my business without interference.

Point Four:

Sugared food is not for me. When will I learn? I scoffed all the sweet treats in the basket as a dessert after dinner last night, and how I've paid for it all day! Such indigestion! I know Mama always said Diabetes runs in our family. I really need to get medical advice on my diet.

Four Points were quite enough. Bored as he so often became, he threw down the quill, heading for the cottage door. Gazing out he smirked a sinister smile, wondering if his Wolf brothers were ready yet to play with him on such a beautiful moonlit night.

A Camino at St Anne's Cathedral

Winding through the lives
the deaths
the remembered
wearing the shell of a pilgrim
the Visitor walks on geometric marbling
soft summer shoes create no sound
into that void the echoes fall
images of colour
light
brightness
hue flicker
but peripheral vision glimpses a shadow
a pass-by from windows of
Patience
Charity
Peace.

the echoes come
not just from past memories
but from the ceremonies of now-
a baby's cry from a christening
a tight sob escaping at a funeral
the shuffling of childish feet
eager to escape the sermon.

as the Visitor walks
layers are stripped
discarded on the floor in tattered shrouds

of the outside
the mundane
the white noise of everyday life

as they drop
a raw core rises
to be stroked by calm essence
hushed grace
a sense of the important truths

in an ambulatory journey
the Visitor is rebirthing
going back into the one soul
the connectivity of humanity
the knowledge of how to be
not what we appear
but what we are.

Breathe and push! let the amoeba pulse and grow.

Rapunzel tresses

Once upon many times…

As prisons go it was better than most. A bedroom, a solar, and a tiny room with a cramped wooden tub and a seat with a runnel to the outside wall, all three areas fitting compact within the circular space at the top of the tower. *A magnificent view from the window in the solar*, her father announced when he left her there, though he had planned that little could be seen from the slits in other two rooms. In the winter months tapestries absorbed the worst of the damp seeping through from the stone walls, and an inadequate brazier sucked some of the chill from the air.

Persinette hauled up a basket with fresh food every morning and a second each evening with coal and kindling, medicaments and manuscripts, clean clothes and hair combs, all that her father deemed necessary for her to maintain *mens sana in corpore sano.* Rainwater was captured in a wooden tank attached to the outside wall, and during the height of the dry summer when rain was scarce, a third basket holding flagons of water was provided each noontide.

Her father had thought of everything - or at least he prided himself he had - for survival but not comfort. That way she'd come to her senses, marry Rupert and their two kingdoms would be joined for evermore. But the girl was stubborn. It had been three years now; she had turned fifteen. If Rupert had not been so blinded by land-lust and his craving for power, he would have looked elsewhere for a bride long ago.

~ ~ ~

The farm was in the middle of nowhere, on the sunless side of a bleak mountain, fit for only sheep and goats. The two fields in which the potatoes and vegetables were grown, had been clawed from the earth by her grandparents, each grey stone excavated by hand, carried with straining shoulders to the field-edge to build boundary walls.

Her father had grown up there, but not much. He was slight, with a curvature of his shoulders resulting from a malnourished childhood and a lack of Vitamin D. Her mother had come from the Foundling Home in the next valley, left there at the door one winters night. She'd been sent to the farm as a worker twelve years from that date, the day of her abandonment designated as her birthday. In time her mother and father married, a logical pragmatic step. As her mother had died giving birth to her, all she knew of her maternal heritage were the scraps she had been told.

She knew almost as little about her father. After her grandparents left him the farm, a passing-over long before her memory could recall, as she grew the two of them spent their days in silence, with only the most necessary of comments about food, the land, the animals. Once years ago when she spoke she heard her voice crack from misuse, so she took care now to talk to the sheep, to the potato shoots, to the flames in the fire, to the strong winds and slight breezes for fear she'd become mute.

The few who visited labelled her strange, but she knew no other way of living. Little did she realise her father planned she never would. Whenever he spoke with others and the subject was raised of her leaving to work elsewhere, or worse of her marriage to some local, he'd describe her strangeness, her feyness, her curious ways. Those who heard this would then stay clear of her, fearing an evil-eyed look or an unexpected curse. Her father had no intention of being left alone on the farm. He knew no second wife could ever be lured here. His few cousins detested the isolation, and the land was too barren to be sold. He was chained to that poor place, and he had decided…so would she be!

~ ~ ~

Crouched on a stool at the rickety table, he could hear his wife snuffling over the plastic basin in the corner. Her tears, escaping in steady drops, added little to the two inches of liquid in the pot. Water was too scarce to waste on washing humans or crockery. The shanty town hut contained nothing as luxurious as a kitchen, just a bench in the corner on which to chop, mash and try to eke out anything edible. Four stones formed an upright rectangle beside it, an insipid fire in their centre, seeping acrid smoke into the already stale air. On the top cross-stone, a pot always boiled, on good days with a liquid which had colour, on poor days an insipid brown. On really good days, when he'd found more cans in the rubbish tip than usual and could buy rice or beans, the liquid became a stew. But it was never enough to fill the five of them - he César, his wife, and the children, Eduardo, Maria and baby Carmelita. Three other childish souls had come and gone, pulling little into their tiny lungs and eating less as they fleetingly passed through their family's threshold.

The Man was due any minute. César turned over the same arguments in his head which he had kneaded many times before. Indeed, he had thought of little else these last weeks. The arrangement was clear. The Man would take Maria, and in return, César would get a job in the factory sorting the cans which others like himself would then bring to him. There would be a weekly wage, enough to keep his family alive, enough to rent a different hut further up the hillside where the air was clearer and Eduardo would cough less, where there was a tap which spat out water, and fewer rats.

He knew of other families who had dealt with the Man, who had in time received letters and photographs proving their little ones were now wives and mothers. The Man was in his own way honourable. He saw his work as charitable, a way for families in the shanty town to survive, and loneliness in distant lands to be eased.

César knew of other more lucrative offers, but also knew that for those girls they ended in shameful lives and early deaths.

A shape filled the doorway, a shadow etched a pattern on the floor. It was time. César surrendered, as he had known he would, to the inevitable. For the last time he called out *Maria, come here.*

~ ~ ~

Those of you with half-empty cups will already have written your own endings.

Those of you with half-full containers, consider these.

Hidden from view, a chivalrous knight had watched the daily proceedings, driven by a noble desire to rescue a prisoner. After many weeks planning, on a certain morning, he knocked out the servant from behind and inserted a long sturdy rope into the basket to be raised. Finding it, she wasted no time in climbing through the solar window and abseiling to the ground. Both were much surprised to see the other, a knight and a young maiden. In the way of such tales, they looked into each other's eyes, married soon after, and lived long and happy lives in a kingdom far away from her father… and from Rupert.

~ ~ ~

In a world where the only two certainties are death and taxes, even as poor a farm as this one, had an official annual visit, seeking a pittance from a pot which didn't exist. Every May a visitor from the Fiscal Department of Taxation would climb the dreary path to the farm half-door. She was just in from the hillside, with her bare brown feet, her cheeks rose-blown by the freshest of air, and her hair wild and free, garlanded with fresh picked daisies. This first sighting, the newly appointed young Clerk would tell their grandchildren, he would never forget until the day the clay covered him.

~ ~ ~

The letter had been read out to them so many times the paper was now as fragile as ancient lace, but her words, dictated to a scribe in Mesquite, near Dallas, had long since been memorised. *He calls me his sinta Papa. He's been learning Tagalog so that the baby and I remember who we are and where we came from. He loves us both so much. I live in a fine house with two bedrooms, a slate roof, and such a grand kitchen! We even have a car. I called the baby César. I think he looks like you.* And indeed, no matter how often the family studied the three photographs, that fact was clear. His daughter grinned at the camera with her mother's eyes, but everyone agreed that his Texan grandson looked exactly like him.

C'mon, you don't believe fairy-tale endings are possible!

seashore living

last night it startled me again

seashore living

gulls lobbed past the window

by a tennis racket wind

grains of sea salt slammed to the glass

etching out a pointillist painting

gusts sleeking the marram like

a model straightening a tight skirt

why does it startle me so

does each withdrawing tide

sand-scrape my memories

leaving only a beached bleached consciousness

Safe Space

He had built the house especially for her. Training to be an architect when they first met, he had always promised that his greatest design would be just for her. At first this was said as a flirtatious tease, but later, after they had fused together, he said, with deep love in his eyes and in his voice, it would be just for them. The tumour put paid to that dream. The house was built, finished just months before he was gone, so he saw its structure, gazed at rooms furnished in her unique style, knew she would live on in comfort. But his essence did not live there long enough to linger. When she walked the rooms now, she heard only her own echoes, felt only her own ripples swirling in the corners of the eaves.

It was truly a masterpiece of a house. In suburban North-East London, passers-by on the street saw only a twenty-foot-high fence of maple, and an entrance camera and buzzer beside solid gates, which were overlain with golden curlicues of copper ivy. Even those who lived in the higher-storied houses nearby, who could see over the fence from their attic rooms, glimpsed only the roof of a single storied dwelling, slanted against pooling rain, and the top of a loggia which veiled most of the garden from overhead view. Inside the building, glass walls, skylights, recessed lighting and reflective surfaces expanded the sense of space and encouraged light to spread and bounce and prism until the eye filled with warmth and the heart glowed.

We will be masters of our castle here, with a drawbridge pulled up behind us… to protect our future little ones, he had smiled as he drizzled champagne from his glass onto the threshold in a christening gesture on the day the building was finished. *You'll be left in a safe space,* he later whispered from his bed in the Hospice. He'd insisted on going there. *I don't want to leave a ghost in the house,* he'd argued. Little could he have realized how much she would long for more residue, more traces of him. His imprint was in every room and line of the building, but the void between the walls now reflected only her hand.

The nursery school welcomed her back that first widowed September. She knew she needed to be out among others during the day, and nursery children asked no prying questions, offered no sympathy which would break her hard-hewn shields. The other teachers soon copied the children. By evenfall she felt filled with enough of the days debris to face a microwaved dinner at the breakfast bar. After that, the wide sofa facing the wall-hung television on which she'd watch 'house design' programmes, savouring words she'd lived with for years. Foundations, scaffolding, insulation. Her life was now empty of these.

By the following April, when the sunlight began to stretch back into the evenings, after her evening meal she took coffee out to the table on the patio. The plants in the earthenware urns spaced throughout the garden had long since begun to yawn and stretch and bud green. Now with increasing vitality and exuberance in the very air around her, she longed for some osmotic tendril of Spring to touch her core, to regenerate life within her. She longed for a spark she feared would never come again.

On the first Monday morning of the summer holidays, as the heat began to rise heavy in the city, she rolled her blue bin onto the pavement. It was far from full, but the weekend heatwave had nudged her sense of smell. The decomposing scraps needed to go. Reaching the kerb, she noted that a child's toy in the gutter must have been thrown in abandon from a passing car. Reaching down to retrieve it for her bin, the furry clump surprised her by first jerking, then whimpering. Not a toy! A hairy, scruffy bundle from which two eyes stared. Anger swept through her. *How could anyone hit an animal and drive on!* Incensed, she forgot to consider the possible repercussions of fleas and other such issues. With great care she lifted the limp mound, and gently carried it to a small square of grass beside the patio. Her first instinct was to try to straighten it out to assess damage. This went well until it came to a tail tightly curled between its back legs. Touching that caused much shivering, and a barely heard yelp.

Now what?

With that thought, she realized that it was already too late to change her course. Without thinking, she had committed herself to being responsible. Using a wet towel from the bathroom and a blanket from the hall closet, she placed a shrouded bundle on the back seat of her car and drove to the veterinary clinic on the High Street. Some hours later, she drove back. The Vet had said that the stitches in the tail would dissolve in about a week and that the bandage should be kept on as long as the dog would allow. He also told her that it was a mongrel about two years old with some collie and spaniel in the mix, who was neither microchipped nor collared and which he therefore suspected was a stray. Battersea Dogs Home told her on the phone not to bring it there as they were so over-crowded, pleaded with her to hold onto it for just a few weeks until they could find a space. She told herself she was a fool when she heard her voice agreeing but knew she could not have left it where she found it.

At a pet superstore on the way back she bought food, dog shampoo, flea and wormer medication. On an impulse she could never rationalize in hindsight, she also threw rawhide treats and a rubber squeaky bone into the shopping trolley. Back at the house, it was bathed, nourished and assigned blanket space on the patio…which lasted for two nights. The third night brought a thunderstorm. As a result, the blanket-bed moved to the kitchen floor. On the fifth evening as it looked up at her while she was heating her tinned soup, she decided that being of more than one variety of breed, it could be called Heinz. After a fortnight had passed, a dog-bed sat beside the sofa in the living room. A month later, on the night she decided she would phone Battersea in the morning to remove him from their listings, as she turned over in bed, her hand dropped down to stroke his smooth silky head. A small lick, and Heinz went straight back to sleep. She smiled into the dark as the metronome of his gentle snoring began again. Architectural design can bring soul and spirit and beauty to a building, but touch and communication and sharing bring a heartbeat.

Oyez! Oyez!

~ an Acrostic~

You listening to me, really listening?
Of course I am!
Until I'm sure you're really listening, I'm not wasting my breath again!
All right, you've my full attention … if it's that important to you.
Really, it is. Your Voice is truly unique. One in seven billion!
Everyone in our Group writes better than me. You know that.

Says you, but it's not true. Your Voice sings the only songs of its own kind ever written.
Pull the other one! Go on, prove it!
Everyone has an individual recipe of ingredients … their childhood, family, life experience
C'mon, everyone's a better background, more schooling, a cleverer brain than me!
It's just different, not better. Who told you *better*?
All the teachers at school, my family, my work colleagues
Like they can touch readers in the way you do!

But they have degrees … and work published … and use clever words … and stuff like that
Every word you write has purity and integrity and power and individuality
Little chance people would take *me* seriously!
I'm telling you again and again, they do!
Exact same answer I'll give you every time. You're talking rubbish
Very well, just why are you so convinced of that?
Each time I read my stuff, it's not good enough! Not compared to the others!

In the end, we've finally got there…..
… the biggest, worst and loudest Critic you have is you!

Secrets and Lies

This piece performed on stage on November 10th, 2022, at a Tenx9 event in Roe Valley Arts Centre in Limavady, Northern Ireland. All stories told at Tenx9 must be autobiographical. The designated theme was 'Secrets and Lies'.

There I was, standing at Derry Airport in the General Reception area, waiting for passengers to disembark from the plane which had just arrived. I had told only two people I would be there, and yet I was not actually keeping it secret. The dark angel from my Catholic upbringing perhaps whispered into my left ear that I could be committing a Sin of Omission, but I preferred to classify it under the CIA umbrella of a 'Those who Need to Know' situation. I had not actually lied to anyone. I had just been uncharacteristically reticent over the last few weeks about what was going on in my life.

So, here's the backstory. At the age of fifty-four I'd been amicably divorced for four years, was well settled in my new home, had started a new business after teaching for 26 years and was now looking for companionship. Four years outside the comfortable corral of 'coupledom' had convinced me that to have any kind of a vibrant social life in Norn Iron, a Plus One was a necessity. How had I reached my fifties without being aware that all social groupings, whether indoors or out on the town, took place in groups of even numbers, never odd ones. I was increasingly coming to the conclusion that the issue with Judas might have had less to do with any cheek-kissing in the Garden of Gethsemane and possibly more to do with the fact that booking an upstairs table for dinner on a Thursday evening would be impossible for a party of thirteen!

Therefore, I did what Singletons the world over now do without batting an eyelid - I joined a dating site. And so back to Secrets and Lies. If anyone had asked back then, I wouldn't have kept it a secret … but of course no one thought to randomly make that enquiry. Ergo I never had to lie. (Cue saintly music from above). But Lordy, Lordy, the secrets I uncovered about certain parts of the rest of these two islands. Now Lisdoonvarna thinks it has it cracked, then and now, as the dating capital of Ireland. It didn't hold a candle when it came to searching for mates to the town of Mullingar. I don't know what the demographic of the town was at that time but going by the number of profiles of single men, I strongly suspected that as every Mullingar-ian female celebrated her eighteenth birthday, the next morning saw her, suitcase in hand, at the bus-stop heading out of town. Nary a male in Mullingar seemed to have a partner.

I don't think it was coincidence that I also discovered at the same time that, in each dating profile in the Category 'Favourite Hobbies', the listed combination of Country Music, John Wayne films and tractors indicted someone with whom I might not have a lot in common. Nothing wrong with any of these interests in the singular! but when linked together they hinted at a conversational scenario in which even I might find myself floundering.

So I looked to the 'other island' to see what the pickings might be like there. What a world of difference in the 'Favourite Hobbies Category '! Was there some kind of secret Senior Olympics being held every four years under my radar? Walking, swimming and cycling were the hobbies of the sloths among the profiles. Any self-respecting male spent his weekends mountain climbing, deep sea-diving and marathon running. I found myself feeling exhausted just reading about them. And yes, the words 'They *must* be lying' did flit across my reality checker. At the very least, I realised that these were not Plus One material … they'd never slow down long enough for me to catch them and test-run them as arm candy.

But my fifty-four-year-old-self had a sense of humour, a wide bandwidth of curiosity and a thran tenacity to continue my Holy Grail search. Practically developing repetitive strain injury in scrolling through page after page of profiles, I kept passing one particularly pleasant smile with a very interesting and appealing description attached. With deep regret I decided to leave a message for this individual. Why regret? he lived in Yorkshire. With no hint of a lie in what I wrote, I saw no reason to keep it a secret that I would have been very interested in this individual had the geographical distance between us been different. He replied in exactly the same open manner. We agreed to email each other occasionally in the future with an update on our online dating progress.

How the Fates must have laughed at our attempts to keep one vital secret from ourselves. We had met our Match - literally. A steady flow of emails and three phone calls followed. This was when, for ordinary folk, Facetime and video calls were still a futuristic fantasy. After a mere eighteen days, he landed on the runway at Derry with his next flight back to Northern Ireland already booked for three weeks hence. We'd never seen anything but a few photos of each other, and the three phone calls had been short… but we knew. We just knew!

It was no secret to anyone who later met us that we were indeed two halves of the one entity, and it remained that way until the moment he passed from oesophageal cancer four and a half short years later. But I don't want this to be a sad tale. That would be a falsity, a lie. I want you to rejoice that this man lived, that we met the way we did, that we loved. It should never be a secret that any couple met on a dating site. After all, who's to judge where the lightning strikes, and love begins.

A Courtyard Garden

The veil was thin in that courtyard garden. Peace, comfortable silence, calm…all the unattainables on the outside of the wall… filtered, slid, slipped through to any who visited. Those who sat there long enough enjoying the stillness, the stoppéd-ness, the centredness, eventually surrendered their fear of the other side of the Great Divide. They were aware of its closeness to their world, were grateful for the gentleness of its presence but were also grateful that it kept its distance.

A round table, two chairs painted Mediterranean blue to match the cottage shutters. Visitors in their passing-through would sit at that table, put down their burdens, let the scented air flow over them soothing their jagged edges. With tumble dryer thoughts stilling, they smelt the passionflower, traced the climb of the clematis, watched the lazy meanderings of bees drunk with potential honey. Indolent cats stretched out beyond lengths belief, tricolour-chests barely rising or falling. Dogs lay in the shade, too content even to pant. When those seated raised their glasses, long stemmed or bulbous, they sipped nectar, feeling their mouths explode with bubbles of joy or letting a velvet deep-red flow tang their throats.

Merely a courtyard in a French Airbnb

… and one level, yes, that's what it was.

But for those who sat at that table it was there they found their Balm from Gilead. Their hearts shimmied. Their souls' core, lost to them outside the walls, was restored.

They were replenished.

They returned time after time

The Saint and the Circle

based on a legend that St Brigid settled a C6th dispute among warriors

She waited

They talked
at each other
over each other
with passion   in anger

She waited

They argued
with the company
into faces spit close
behind other's backs

She waited

They spoke
in high rhetoric
or with snaps   snarls
and many clipped curses

She waited

They grew tired
their throats hurt
their heads ached
their tongues burned

She waited

The space between sounds   stretched   into   silence

She spoke then

She spoke
with quiet dignity
in measured tones
her words resonating
her voice soothing their fire

They shuffled their feet
dropped rigid shoulders
opened closed hearts
heard as they hadn't before
saw the sense of it

One by one they nodded
leaving the circle
in quiet acquiescence
her own gentle might
had prevailed again

The Journey

This piece was performed on stage on February 23rd, 2023, at a Tenx9 event as part of The Steinbeck Festival in Roe Valley Arts Centre in Limavady, Northern Ireland. All stories told at Tenx9 must be autobiographical. The designated theme was 'The Journey'.

Right now, brace yourself Folks! For all you pet-lovers out there, to paraphrase Bette Davis in the 1950 film 'All about Eve', "Fasten your seat belts...it's going to be an emotional bumpy night". In my best Air-hostess voice, Kleenex are available at my table for parts of this journey, and air-punching is positively encouraged for other stages en route.

My much beloved and irreplaceable Brown Dog was taken to the Vets for the last time on July 31st last year. Her generous heart could finally take no more. She had remained three years after the Vet gave his Prognosis of '*only a year at most*' when her heart condition was first diagnosed. Had she some precognition that in March 2020 the world as we knew it, would come to a halt, and the word 'isolating' would come to have a poignant depth of meaning, previously unbelievable to we two-legs? Well anyway, she'd decided she was going nowhere, was staying to see me through this, and we passed the Bubble time together in my Portstewart flat, keeping each other company.

But on July 31st last year her journey stopped. She'd got me through the worst of it. She could now leave. She went. I'd a major book event happening on November 20th so while I mourned very very deeply, I kept myself busy with organizational activities, and ignored, as best I could, the emptiness in the flat. The Event came and went, and by the end of November I could ignore the situation no longer. I needed a new canine. Never a replacement, that was impossible! but it was time to welcome an entirely new entity.

All my adult life every animal I ever owned was a Rescue one. In fact, as time went on, I would deliberately seek out dogs and cats who were emotionally damaged. I would consider the end of each long rehabilitation period from which they emerged feeling safe and loved, as a triumph for Humankind. I began looking at the Rescue Centres all over Northern Ireland full of those poor animals adopted when people had worked from home, and which were now abandoned (agreed, sometimes very unwillingly) when the world kick-started itself.

Thus in December, another Journey began…in true Literary tradition, a Grail Quest. I felt well equipped for the Rescue Mission. My Qualifications? Having returned to Norn Iron six years ago from living in France, I now resided in a flat in Portstewart. With a huge Green right at my Building's front door and beaches everywhere one looked, there would be an endless variety of stimulating walks. I had decades of experience with Rescue Animals. I now had the extra time of the retired to care for a pet, and having taken up Writing much of my Leisure time was spent at home where I could keep the animal company. I wanted, not a puppy but an older dog, which were always harder for Centres to rehome. I wasn't fussy about sex or breed, open to all suggestions. Furthermore, I was determined not to buy a pet from an ad site, thus feeding into the culture of puppy farming, which I loathe with a passion. And…there was a definite space in my emotional life ready to be filled.

The first week in December saw the beginning of the Social Media Stage of my Journey-Quest. On Facebook, I joined the sites of every Northern Irish Rescue Centre, confident that with my background, the open bandwidth of my requirements and the constant cry of over-crowding from the Animal Websites themselves, I'd have a companion for Yule Week. And back came the same uncompromising reply from every single Centre - there was one thing I didn't have, an outdoor space with a six-foot-high enclosing fence. At first I half agreed with this idea. Of course, it made sense that the large dogs I didn't want to own such as huskies and Alsatians, could, if necessary, have a safe place to play unsupervised. The other half of me chortled however, conjuring up images of pole-vaulting yorkies and chihuahuas, toy poodles and westies hurling themselves at, and hopefully over, six-foot-high fences. Why was such a high fence needed for *them*? Perhaps a new Adventure Category for Crufts I thought!

After a week of consistently the same response, I wondered if the compulsory requirement of a high enclosed outdoor space was to do with toileting. But Brown Dog and I had visited the Green every two hours, and it was never a problem. By the end of the second week, I wondered was there some inherent issue with apartment living? A quick Google Search confirmed that there were 600,000 dogs living in New York City, with one pet for every three households. Did the Rescue Centres in Northern Ireland think that all the dog owners in Manhattan were unfit? It wasn't just me falling short then!

By the time the festivities started in earnest at the end of December, my hopes could not have been lower. My flat, it seemed, was not good enough. Rules were Rules. No exceptions were considered. It was a very miserable, despairing end of Year. Over-worked devoted volunteers on Rescue Centre Facebook Pages were writing heart-breaking stories of overcrowding, fearing the onset of the 'rejected presents' to come. But Rules were apparently Rules.

Of all things, mobile phone algorithms came to my rescue. Due to my month spent scanning for canines, up popped an unexpected ad for a dog, *'free to the right home'*. Kleenex at the ready alert! John in Belfast had been diagnosed in December with COPD in both lungs, and had to give up his much-loved show beagle of only three years of age. Respecting your tear ducts, I'll keep this short. I went to Belfast. I was interviewed. I was declared fit. John's eyes filled with tears as he lifted his pretty little beagle into the back of my car. (I warned you this might be sad!) She came home with me. I've since sent him many photos and updates, and he doesn't regret his choice of new owner for a second.

I can now report that this 'rescued' beagle and her new owner have commenced a very happy life together (cue air-punching). We've learned that she doesn't need an enclosed back yard with a six-foot fence. She just wants to be loved, as do I.

a canine acrostic

~ a dog walk when it is snowing ~
(Human - English, Canine - translation provided)

And you wanted to come out in this!
Don't blame me. If I've to pee, I've to pee.
Oh, that ole line. Why can't you just cross your paws!?!
God, when will you learn, I've only a tiny bladder. I've held on as long as I can.
Well, it's not long enough. I was very comfortable in that armchair doing the Crossword.
All right, I'll go on the carpet the next time.
Like you did last week?
Kitchen door was shut or I'd have gone on the tiles. We both know that's easier to clean.
Well, you didn't. I was on my knees for hours with the steamer and hairdryer.
Her daft idea, buying that thick white carpet.
Ever consider she only choose a Pomeranian so the hairs wouldn't show?
Nope. One look at me and she was in love. Just like you.
I fell in love? That's drastically overplaying it, don't you think. You're still on probation.
That Back-to-the-Dealer threat wore thin weeks ago. You know you love me.

In this weather! Don't push your luck.

So, what, you're a bit wet and cold? Just look at how gorgeous I am in my fur coat.

Soaked to the skin, me. Probably get my death.

Now stop being such a drama queen. We'll be back at the House in a few minutes.

Out in this weather for an ungrateful mutt like you. I must be mad!

Would you rather be stuck with just her Sphinx cat as a pet!?!

It certainly seems a better option at the moment.

Now look, we're back at the Front Door. You can stop whinging.

Get inside. That's your last walk today. No, don't look at me with that smirking smile. This time I mean it.

Samhain Seeds

~ The Stimuli prompt~

Seeds I would like to plant for others in the future

an open threshold
a warm heart
an unfettered soul
a peaceful centre
a soothed mind
an ease of saying
a quiet of listening
a nurturing touch
a sheltering arm
a raft of support
a bridge to move forward
a cleansing of shadow
a tendril of connection
an embrace of safety
a caress of caring
a place to rest
a rejoicing of success
a heartbeat of plenty
a gift for you
a giving for me

Footnote: *Written at a Course called 'Samhain Seeds' given by Dearbhaile Bradley, November 2022 for the feast of Samhain.*

A clock ticks

~after The Black Marble Clock

by Paul Cezanne, 1870 ~

The Clock ticked on…

Much as she wanted to reject the obvious truth, as the hour hand approached eleven, she had to accept he wasn't coming. He was always punctual to a fault. The hours between Nine and Twelve every Thursday morning were hers. His wife believed that was the time of his weekly Inspection of the warehouse in La Villette, the newly created 19th Arrondissement. Instead, he visited the apartment he rented there for Colette.

She looked around the room in despair. The tattered chaise lounge, the spindly table draped in a much-washed piece of faded linen, a few cheap vases. The only bright colour came from the conch shell he'd brought at a market stall in Montmartre. A trip made during the first heady weeks of attraction, that had been the only expedition he had risked outside the apartment. After all, Montmartre was a district of Paris where he was convinced no-one of his *ton* would see them together. Only the riff raff seeking cabarets and brothels went there. He became more cautious. After that, they stayed behind closed doors.

The black marble clock was the only thing of value in the room. He'd given it to her a few weeks after his visits began. *You'll know now the exact time when I'm yours, and yours alone.* She'd spent the last few sous of his weekly allowance on a lemon. He preferred his tea with lemon. A single cup only set out on the table. She was too sick in the mornings to face even tea. Had she misread his reaction last week when she'd broken her news? He'd gone very quiet, very still. She had thought it was shocked delight. After all, his wife had never been able to give him a child. As the hour hand moved towards noon, for the first time she wondered had that perhaps been his preference, not his wife's misfortune.

When the last of the twelve echoing chimes faded into silence, she was forced to a decision. She'd have to sell the clock. It would give her the train fare back to Lisle, back to the small auberge her parents ran there. She began a prayer to Le Bon Dieu. *Please let my parents welcome me …and the baby.*

…and in a different time, a different place, the clock ticked on

It must be her imagination. The tick of the black marble clock could not be getting louder. Her nerves stretched, she told herself she must be imagining it. IT sat on top of the ormolu fireplace, contrasting with its gilt bronze colouring. . Both items had been hard to source even with her extensive list of connections. But Jen would have only the best around her.

Her apartment might be a penthouse in Manhattan but once through its front doors visitors were transported to the Paris of the Second Empire. If a furnishing could not have been appreciated by Napoleon III himself, it had no place in her life. Throughout her apprenticeship in Sotheby's New York on the Upper East Side, she'd been drawn to French furnishings, a pull which solidified into a particular love for the decor of the 1860s and 70's. She could not explain why at the time.

Later, a chance remark by a friend led her to a firm of Genealogists who confirmed that in his 40s the son of her French great great-grandmother had emigrated to America around the turn of the 20th century. Since hearing that, Jen had honoured that heritage by furnishing her apartment à *la française* and signing her full birth name Genevieve, the patron saint of Paris.

On leaving Sotheby's to become a dealer in French antiques, she was delighted to go into partnership with Gene, a fellow Sotheby's apprentice. His strength lay however in Merchandising and Accounts. He appreciated the furniture, the vases, the ornate Empire style in which she delighted, but for him the items translated into dollars and cents. He loved what was most sellable, his favourite sound being the ker-ching of the till. The partnership worked well. He gave her freedom in the buying for, and stocking of, Chez Paris, the Showroom at 726, Sixth Avenue. At the back of New York Tiffany, it still had a salubrious address but a lower ground rent and much more space than most Fifth Avenue stores. She, in turn, gave him full freedom with the books and accounts, trusting him without reserve.

One night the reason for this trust burst into the open. Too much wine at a Staff party, stoked by a mutual satisfaction with a very prestigious sale, found them waking up the next morning in her bed. Over coffee and croissants at her breakfast bar he confessed his long-standing love for her. She acknowledged later to her bathroom mirror that she'd been aware of it, indeed had traded on it but, while she had enjoyed the sex and valued him as a business partner, he was not her idea of a lifetime soulmate. Much to her relief she was leaving that day on a pre-planned six-week tour around Europe searching for stock. She would not have to face him anytime soon, except for business emails and the occasional Zoom. He would not push for more until her return. It was not his way.

So now here she sat six weeks later, listening to the ticking of the black marble clock. He was due to arrive at her front door at any minute. She, in control of so much of her life, had no idea of how the ensuing conversation would go. She had already decided to get rid of it. She had a business to run, a full and focused life. If only he would see the sense of that! But what if he didn't? There was a serious possibility he might want her to keep it, would break-up the partnership if she disposed of it. She was realistic enough to accept she'd never find such an efficient and co-operative Associate again. She began to take deep concentrated breaths, chant the mantra her therapist had taught her. *Trust the Universe to provide the best outcome.*

Some summers are different.

~ a homage to our ancestors who survived so that we do ~

The Year of Our Lord, 1348, this summer differs to those which have gone before. A London peddler brought The Black Death to our small cluster of villages in the valley. Stopping on his way north he spread out his treasures at the May Fair, his ribbons and laces, such sweet carriers of death. The young maidens fell first, killed by the desire to look fetching or slain by a token from a love-sick suitor. Then the babies and toddlers, the pregnancy-drained mothers and in the end, with inevitable fatal advance, we men. Crimson rosettes budded on skin like florescent petals, red Crosses bloomed on afflicted doorposts, grimmer summer flowerings than those known before.

Last summer had passed in long heat-heavy days, filled from dawn to dusk with the annual duress of coercing survival from the land. We tasted the sweetness of wild blackberries and raspberries. We watched our stock fatten and flourish. At September's end, that Harvest feasting had been such a celebration of summer abundance. We had toasted it with rich honey mead and strong full-bodied beer made from sturdy hops. Such a backbreak of toil but we knew we would survive the winter, were joyous in that knowledge.

This summer we few who survive, weak as we are, battle uphill in these dark days. The stock is all which now thrives, roaming free on the land, eating forbidden delights; the sweetest of grasses, the fattest fallen nuts. The smell of Death fills our nostrils. At night the bone-fires of the days' departed taint the air with the tang of burning meat, making our treacherous stomachs twist and growl. We drag ourselves to the hay meadows, scything and stooking what we can, but know it will not be enough for us all. Surviving the buboes has not been enough. Ahead lies the spectre of a winter's slow starvation.

Yes, some summers are different to others.

A Fox Unearthed

"He is like the fox, who effaces his tracks in the sand with his tail." – Niels Henrik Abel

Who hadn't heard of Nick Fox, the darling of the silver screen! No self-respecting period drama had been made on either side of the Pond in recent years without his handsome profile, thespian vowels and charismatic manner enhancing its appeal to the general public. By the age of thirty-six he was box-office gold… and he knew it!

Unlike some others however, his only mission in life was to stay at the top of the cinematic tree for as long as possible. No film star lifestyle for him! Only the discreetest of affairs, no dallying with the wives, daughters or girlfriends of anyone who might have the power to blacklist him. Moreover, his body was subjected to the most stringent of diets and daily rigorous workouts with the much acclaimed 'Personal Trainer to the Stars' Taekwondo Black Belt, Antoine Perry.

Furthermore, of all the candidates for the position of PA which the Recruitment Agency had sent him at the time of his first major success - and its accompanying Oscar nomination for his portrayal of Mr Darcy - he chose Hepzibah Weston, a dour religious Fundamentalist who, like Cerebus at the Gates of Hell, controlled his social diary and media representation with the full repressed passion of the desiccated spinster she already was by her early thirties. She'd only applied for the post in order to save his soul from the temptations of being a rich and famous celebrity.

Finally, Sam Snead, his Voice Coach, had long since ironed out any background twang from his childhood, and trained his voice to mimic that of either the highest ranking aristocratic of the English Upper Crust or the most Brahmin of the Bostonian First families. Old World, New World, he could speak with ease in either tongue.

As his parents had died in a car crash from which he in his Moses basket had been rescued, when no other family came forward, he had been taken in and raised by a previously unknown Aunt Minnie. The *Mighty Mouse* was her billing. Less than five feet tall, it was claimed she could raise her own body weight above her head. Regardless of the fact that the weights she used were obviously fake, no one challenged the ferocious little murine of the truth of this, fearing her wrath. Small she might have been in stature, but she packed a mighty punch.

As he had grown up living in her caravan, moving from circus to circus, when she died just after his eighteenth birthday, there was no-one left who remembered his origins, his background. So, after careful thought, he decided to obliterate his roots forever. Having passed his teenage years soaking up Entertainment Today magazines, he changed his name by deed poll to one he felt would best suit the siren call he could no longer resist, to become an actor - or better yet, a film star. From time to time, he would smile a private smile to himself. Now he was the only soul in the entire world who knew his original name … and that was a secret he was never going to share!

The latest project he had just started filming was the hybrid lovechild of a P G Wodehouse novel and an Agatha Christie whodunnit. He, as an aristocratic sleuth in the 1920's, was going to solve a murder case by weeding out the killer among the Christmas weekend house guests on a grand estate in the Cotswolds. The first scene was very straight-forward. In it, the sleuth's butler, Clarence Cogwick, had gone ahead to arrange adjoining rooms for Nick's character, named Binky Foster, and Binky's best friend Farquhar Arbuthnott. While Clarence bustled around unpacking travelling bags in the background, he and Farquhar were to stare out the window, in order to assess the charms of the three nieces of their host. They, giggling and carefree, were spilling out of the Silver Ghost which had just pulled up in front of the balustrade at Royam Hall. The type of scene he could do on autopilot. And he did! *It's a wrap,* the Director shouted after the second take, smiling broadly at Nick. This was why he was so popular. Everyone loved to work with such a consummate professional.

The next scene required more complicated staging. The most attractive of the three nieces - and his scripted love interest - was played by an up-and-coming ingénue named Penelope Fellows. In this scene, the first they were to film together, he had to follow her onto a balcony to continue his romantic pursuit, away from the other drawing room guests. The scene, being filmed in twilight, was a complicated exercise in lighting. As the two of them stood side by side outside the French windows, shivering with cold, little was said. By the time the Director asked them to stand together in a tight embrace so that the 'Sparks' could adjust their lights, high and low, soft-focus and glaring, their teeth were chattering so much they could barely speak. Therefore, it sideswiped Nick completely when his co-star whispered into his ear:

I know who you are, and what you came from.

Frozen into immobility now as much by shock as by the bitter night air, his mind raced. What could she mean? And if she did mean what he feared, then was she going to reveal everything? This would shatter the current complacent life he had built on an effective web of lies drawn up by his Publicity Agent. The alternative version of his background was built upon fictitious middle-class parents, a stable but uneventful childhood, and a random break at a teenage audition, attended with his mates just for a laugh. Both only children, those parents too had 'died' in a car accident, the childhood home had been 'flattened' in a city re-generation project, the school 'closed' on absorption into a single district comprehensive. With his legal name-change all those years ago, there could be no alternative paper trail for eager fans to excavate, not to mention the sleazier tabloids. He'd ensured a cold trail. There was no possibility of the truth being revealed. And yet! she'd said what she had. Recovering as fast as this train of thought would allow, Nick tried to parry her statement.

What do you mean, Pen?

His acting skills enabled him to drawl these words in a nonchalant way his character, Binky Foster, would have envied.

My real name's Rhapsody McDuff. My father employed your aunt for a season.

With horror he realised she was speaking the truth. The summer he was fourteen, he and Minnie had toured Ireland with McDuffs circus. It had been a proud summer for Minnie. McDuffs Circus, established three centuries earlier, was one of the oldest in the world. With increasing pressure to ban animal acts, they had hired more and more of the type of acts known as 'Barnum and Bailey Spectaculars'. Minnie's act had slotted right in. He himself had been taken on as a general helper, working especially with the trapeze equipment. He had no fear of heights, a necessary prerequisite for fixing the swings and bars high in the tent top. He remembered a curly haired child, who'd followed him round the ring. And yes, she'd had a ridiculous name. John McDuff, her father, had loved Gershwin's *Rhapsody in Blue,* and had insisted on her Christian name. It had been a joke among the Irish circus hands who'd re-named her Soda.

He realized the folly of trying to brazen it out. This was his co-star for the next eleven weeks of filming. He'd never be able to focus on his acting and successfully maintain a string of lies at the same time. A pragmatist he surrendered, whispered into her ear.

So, you're little Soda. Are you going to tell? What would make you keep quiet?

At that moment the Director instructed them to position themselves for the first run-through of the scene. Nick stumbled through the lines, missing the cues, blurring the nuances. The Director and crew could not believe it. This was Nick Fox! The One-Take Wunderkind. His stunt double could have played the part better. What was wrong? Blaming the cold - that long wait in the night air while the lighting was being adjusted - Nick asked if he and his co-star could have a half-hour break in their trailers … just to heat up. He'd be fine if he was warm. With reluctance, the Director agreed, muttering under his breath about production costs and lost time.

Once off the set, Nick moved quickly. As soon as he thought would seem natural to passing on-lookers, he knocked on the trailer door marked *Penelope Fellows*. He had to know. Was his world safe? Tense with a fear he was trying to repress, he was less urbane than usual.

Well, wh- what are you going to do?

Nothing of course, Nick. It's no-one's business but your own. I was just letting you know I knew.

But …? You mean …. ? Nothing???

Well, they're already talking about a sequel for this film. If they go down that route, you could maybe put in a good word for me. Your voice carries clout.

That's all? A good word?

Why are you so surprised? I don't get it!

As indeed she didn't. The movie world was a cut-throat one. She could have black-mailed him for the rest of his life. Could she be that rarest of finds, a genuinely good soul, in the often-seedy world of the silver screen? He asked himself that question many times over the following year. The last time it crossed his mind was as he stood in the small private Church on Maui watching her walk up the aisle towards him. Only the two of them knew that in the future she would not really be Mrs Fox, but would in fact be Mrs……..!

Footnote: *At the November 2022 Launch of her books 'The Kingdom' and 'Springboards: a creative Writing Manual', Mary Farrell held a competition in which audience members would post fictitious names into a bowl. The name drawn at the end of the Launch would feature in a future story. This is that story. Is the name your creation? More than one entry was used in this tale about names and naming.*

Shaped

~ after 'I Come from' by Robert Seatter, 2006 -

I came from

a long long long list of don'ts:
don't play with the council children
don't get your socks dirty
don't make a mess
don't risk the angered face
with thin lips and obelisk stare

I came from

a place of relentless cold where:
hips were bared to the sally rod
second was just not good enough
judgement pierced like jagged rocks
lying was a survival skill
kindness was a lapse

I came from

a place of silence where:
the radio was never on
playing was without noise
laughter was unexpected
soft words shrivelled unsaid
The Rules never needed repeating

programmed

reprogrammed

I come from

a sanctum where hearts:
praise til souls swell within
cherish within caring arms
push   pull   carry over mountains
soak up tears with gentle murmurs
soothe with a balm of tenderness

I come from

a battleground of 'you can' where:
the charge is always positive
succeeding is a lance forged in firm flame
defeated is an invalid concept
martyr and victim are ugly forbidden words
I fight self-bound to Cuchulainn's stone

Just stop…think!

Loretta bit her lip…painfully. It was becoming harder and harder to say nothing. She'd known Desiree for so long, since their first day together at Rokewold Infants to be precise. Okay, they'd not been close after Desiree moved to a different District when she married, but it was beginning to seem it would be impossible to sustain any degree of friendship with her in the future. When had she become so self-centred, so unaware of the chaos and cruelty she was strewing round her every time she opened her mouth? School Reunions had their ups and down, everyone knew that. The 32nd Annual Reunion in the Assembly Hall of Southbank High was not expected to be any different, but no-one could have predicted this level of devastation. So, all because of the unstoppable stream of comments from just one person.

To Tracey - *I hear he left you. And for a barmaid with three kids. You're better off without him!*

To Irwin – *Honey, your Mama was bed-ridden for so long, you should be glad she's not suffering any more.*

To Sherie – *College isn't for everyone, I always say. If that boy of yours feels he'll get more outta back-packing round the world, then good for him.*

To Nelson – *Now don't you fret that your company's*

starting to lay off workers. You'll always get another job, you're not that old yet.

And it went on… and on… and on! As she moved round the room chatting loudly to her old classmates, she left them scarred, wounded, bleeding internally. Something had to be done. Loretta waited for the right moment, then grabbed Desiree by the arm just as she was about to move onto another victim. Frogmarching her out of the Assembly Hall, she bustled them both into a nearby Science Classroom. Hands on her hips she launched into an angry tirade, about discretion and empathy, about understanding and kindness, about all the remarks Desiree should never have made, about how she should have stopped and thought before she spoke.

Eventually she ran out of steam. She stopped ranting and looked at Desiree to see if any of what she had said had registered. She was bewildered by what she saw. Desiree seemed to have shrunk, her shoulders were bowed, her lips trembling. At the same instant, both decided to sit, sinking onto a nearby graffiti-ed chipped lab bench.

Well, have you anything to say for yourself?

Desiree reached up her sleeve, pulling out a tissue. It took two false starts before she could speak.

I didn't realise, truly I didn't. I haven't seen everyone in so long. You all must have noticed I've not been to a Reunion for three years now. I…I…I just couldn't face you all. Things have gone so wrong. Steve walked out, another woman. Then two months later Mama passed. The following May my baby boy, my Lewis, decided he'd move to the Coast to get a job near somewhere he could surf at the weekends. And then the house was empty, far too big for just me. Not that it mattered in the end, I couldn't keep up the payments on a house that size by myself anyway. It had to go. And when the Wilsons retired and closed their bakery, I lost my wages from there. Got a new job as a live-in housekeeper on the other side of the river. I live there now in a flat over the garage. I thought that, as I knew what it felt like to go through these things, I could encourage everyone, show them they weren't alone. If I can keep going day after day, they can too. But it's been hard Loretta, so so hard! I know that better than most! I was just trying to…

…and with that, she broke down completely, trying to wipe away tears with a tissue now far too damp to absorb any more moisture.

Loretta was stunned. She hadn't known any of this. She realised she hadn't registered that Desiree had not been at the last three Reunions. She hadn't known about Steve leaving. Like all her friends she'd complained when the Wilson bakery downtown had closed two years ago. Where would she get such delicious cakes in the future, not to mention their beautiful French loaves? It hadn't occurred to her to think about any staff they might have employed. She never drove through the District Desiree had moved to, would never have seen a For Sale sign, nor looked at the Obituary Notices from the local Churches.

But worse, she realised she hadn't tried to know. She had simply forgotten all about Desiree, who'd played no part in her busy social world of family, work, the Church at weekends. She'd let her slip through the slats of her life.

Whose turn was it now to stop and think!

her new whiskey bottle

~ after 'Labelled with Love',

sung by Squeeze, 1981 ~

she unscrews the top of her new whiskey bottle
sniffs brown velvet Lethe   tantilizing respite
a slow steady onset into kindly oblivion
a cracked clouded glass is filled to its rim
shunning the pretention of inch high shots
liquored bloodstream the aim why bother to
posture
who cares it's the taste of the cheapest bought
she seeks anaesthetic   solace sought

since he's been gone she feels owed some reprieve
from the pain of his absence   being a reject ex-wife
blunted sounds filter in from an outside street
underlining the pain of a lonely heartbeat
the power of the malt pads the walls of her world
blurs the prison hours passed on the edge of a knife
she freefalls into sleep   dark insensate empty
but each morning wakes up to again unscrew
the top of her new whiskey bottle.

Footnote: *Written in response to the Stimulus: Write song lyrics based on the first line of an actual song*

Just who the hell *are* you?

(Supermarket Tannoy Voice heard at intervals in the background)

Well hello there, fancy meeting you here!
Hi there… and how are you? Oh, I shop here all the time. Great vegetarian section.
Wouldn't know. To be fair, the wife always did the shopping, but now I'm off on the sick….
You must find it strange these days with all that time on your hands.
Well, they did say I could be back at work the end of next month if everything was okay.
And how could they be sure about that? You don't want to go back too soon.
I've an appointment with the Consultant. It'll be his call.
You're looking really great considering all you've been through.
It was a hard time now, right 'nough.
Have you any lingering side effects?
Nope, I've been really really lucky. Just a bit tired now and again in the evenings.
So you're over all the other problems?
Oh yeah, the operation dealt with them all.
All of them? But some of them must have been really hard to deal with?
Well, it was a four-hour procedure.
Is that how long it normally takes?

That's what they told me.

And how long were you in the hospital all together?

From the time I was rushed in, nearly three weeks. The operation, then two weeks recovery.

Bet your wife was really shocked when you needed to be rushed in.

Well, obviously I knew nothing about how she was doing. I was totally out of it.

You mean there were no clues at all before that? No warning signs? Nothing?

Not a thing! One minute fit as a flea, the next I was coming to in the ambulance.

Do they say you might need to have any more treatment now… in case it happens again?

Nope, the operation dealt with everything. They told me just to maybe take it a bit easier.

Will you be able to do that when you go back to work?

Oh yeah, the staff there have been great, so supportive. Talking about shorter shifts an' all!

Well, I'll see you there in a month's time then. Really really great talking to you! Bye!

I wanna live before I die

~ a sensual bucket list ~

(after a line in 'Live before I die', sung by Marina Kaye, October 2015)

Again before I die…

I want to see:

cloudless domed skies, distant heat-shimmer horizons, an Aurora Borealis of psychedelia, crocheted villages of white cottages with sea blue shutters, golden eagles hang glide, crazy sunsets and exploding sun rises

I want to hear:

booming waterfall thunder, giggling toddlers, ancient ballads, distant panpipes, the words 'I love you', the roar of many planes leaving many runways, excited chatterings in oriental queues

I want to smell:

the overwhelm of passionflower, Eastern temple incense,
sheep lanolin on my fingers, the freedom of escape,
Stateside taxi leather, baby powder on new-born cheeks,
my love's scent on his shirt

I want to taste:

a salt sting in sea air, undulating pasta swirl in my
mouth, the aftermath of laughter, a crisp crunch of salads,
joy in hard-fought success, market stall fresh herbs, an
apero cocktail ice cube

I want to touch:

sun-warmed skin, tight-hold-on fingers, the smooth ears
of many dogs, the curve of a deep smile, warm sand
tween my toes, new bought virgin sheets, the hearts of
others

…then I'll know I've lived

Once valued …!

Just when the little Schoolhouse thought things could not get worse, a shabby lorry arrived, disgorging men with vexatious energy, loud shouting and worst of all, sharp tools. She'd little enough ragged covering for her bony rafters and wind-whipped stones, but when they started to scrape out the meagre filling left between the spaces of her outer shell, she knew she'd reached the end of her tolerance. She could no longer hold together, felt the last threads of her steadfastness crumble.

It had been too long since the children left, her doors finally closing. For years she'd been such a feature for the Estate children, even the girls. The Old Master had been open-minded and liberal, declaring that all his workers' children deserved to know their letters and numbers. And where better for them to learn about their Lord and the Empire than at a school desk! The Sunday School teacher had her hands far too full with all of the children of the town fisher folk. And after all, the little ones pulled what weight they could each planting and harvest-tide.

Emilia Wilson, daughter of the Estate Manager, fulfilled her Christian Duty three mornings a week by teaching the children the Three R's, whilst also monitoring their hygiene and thus improving their health. After the first lessons, held in one of the farm buildings, Lady Caroline, a noble woman in every moral fibre of her being, had insisted a Schoolhouse be built. A single rectangular room contained a black potbellied stove against the inside of the back wall, with separate stone cubicles leaning against the outside of the same wall to preserve decency when Nature called. Two symmetrical windows framed the doorway, narrow to prevent draughts. Also, for protection, the Schoolhouse was constructed near the Main Gate in a glade among mature sturdy trees whose branches and leafage for most of the year mitigated the worst of the Atlantic costal weather.

How the little Schoolhouse had proudly watched the progress of every pupil. She saw them grow strong and tall, warmed to their laughter as they played during the mid-morning recess. Running, jumping, throwing, catching, the energy of youth flowed in them. She sighed a little each time a pupil left forever, tucking under their elbow a brown embossed Bible aimed to guide them through adulthood. She tried to stretch taller on twilit summer evenings when some would meet at her back wall, hiding them from the view of those passing by from the farm or the road. She pretended not to hear their murmurings, tried not to eavesdrop on their nuzzlings but would rejoice on those certain Sundays when she would see nosegays and bouquets gathered from the hedgerows being joyfully carried down Church Road to the sound of ringing bells.

Time does bring change however. The Family spent less and less time at the Big House, preferring City life and milder climes. Machines could now do the work of ten. Many families had been forced into factory life far away. Regular autobuses could shuffle the few remaining children into the new School in the town with its three classrooms, built in response to the rapid growth in local population since the turn of the century. The little Schoolhouse was no longer needed, its door and windows boarded over. It shrank into a lonely life, its roof disintegrating, walls mossing over and playground markings fading.

The worst change happened after the Summer of the Storms. Unexpectedly one summer, like a Biblical punishment, storm followed storm throughout a two-month period. Strong winds, fierce rains and cruel lightning shards attacked the trees around the little building, which crouched shaking under the onslaught. That Autumn any trees which had not already succumbed to Natures might, were felled. She'd lived all her life with the sounds of rooks, busy and bustling in their untidy nests. The glade was suddenly gone, the air caw-silent. The little Schoolhouse now stood unprotected, naked. Her dereliction was seen by all. Over the next few months, her roof sank, her walls shrivelled inwards in shame.

Then the following Spring, the men came, poking, prodding. They cut and scraped and sliced at her until she knew she could take no more. As she lost heart her screams faded into shuddering sobs and finally into barely heard whimpers.

Wait .... what's this?

The men had begun to rub some kind of salve into her wounds. They attached frames for her walls to lean upon and placed crutches under her crossbeams. Each day provided some new nourishment, strengthened her a little more. A new roof, snug window frames, a strong wooden door sheened green. A pebbled path curved in from the roadside. She smiled at her own joyful vanity when they painted the woodwork edging her eaves. Best of all, tall saplings were planted around her in a circle, whispering of future shelter and comfort as they swayed and shimmied in the early May sunlight.

She was a little bewildered by the very last task of the workmen. They attached a wooden sign to her front wall beside the door, and erected a similar one at the roadside beside the Gatehouse. Both had markings. After they left, everything packed in the lorry, even scruffier now, she wondered what the next day would bring.

A bus full of schoolchildren, that's what it brought! The doors sliding open they poured out, jostling, giggling, full of life. At the same time, a small blue car turned into the drive. A young woman emerged. Rosy cheeked, hair escaping from a thick bouncing ponytail, she marshalled the children into a semicircle around the front door in order to take a photograph.

Congratulations! You're the very first group to visit the Cromore School Museum.

The rest of the day passed in a whirl of glee for the little Schoolhouse. She chuckled along when the children laughed. She clapped when they pirouetted in their costumes - truth to tell more familiar clothes she remembered school children wearing than those they had worn getting off the bus. She nodded approvingly when the young woman - Miss Doherty she heard the children call her - made them tidy up all the discarded wrappings from their lunches into a large bag which was stored on the bus to be taken away. It had been such a sunny day they had eaten on the grass outside. She sighed a constricted little sigh after the bus left when Miss Doherty locked the front door again with a large black key. It had been such a treat to have children to cosset again.

Miss Doherty did not leave at once. Instead, she sat down on one of the two benches the workmen had placed on either side of the front door. She leaned back, closed her eyes and turned her face up to the last rays of the May sunshine. *I'm going to love coming here every day, the perfect job for me.* Hearing this, the little Schoolhouse felt her walls expand with warmth, her painted eaves reflect the glow of the evening light. *Every day!* She too thought it was the most perfect way Miss Doherty could share her days to come.

Tramped in the Gutter

The man with the grey eyes gazed down at the filthy heaped jumble at his feet. Lying on plastic bags to keep out the damp from the dark concrete doorway, the bottom half was wrapped in a frayed hessian sack, the top swaddled in a torn tarpaulin like a supermarket chicken. Standard combat uniform for the homeless. The oblivion for yet another freezing night had been sucked from the empty bottle of Buckies, which rolled into the gutter when the mound twitched despite its coma-like stupor.

Well, you've a job to do. You promised yourself, so get on with it!

Reaching down under the right shoulder of the unkempt beggar to lift him, the situation changed in an instant. The figure began jerking as if electrified. Clutching grimy rags to a meagre form, eyes wide and terrified, he strafed the air with panicked cries.

Wadda you doin'? Stealing ma stuff. Leave me be!

But the stranger continued to lift, pulling with all his weight on the man's right shoulder to bring the figure upright. Too befuddled to fight with any coherence or strength, the tramp was half carried, half dragged to an open doorway in the next street.

We'll give you food, dry clothes, a bed for the night.

You're gonna do what? Why?

With a gentle smile, the man from Samaria with the grey eyes explained.

There's always help for everyone under my roof.

Izzy & Adam

It was only natural to want to know more about him. From behind slanted conservatory blinds, at 2.15 every afternoon, Izzy Bellamy watched him walk along behind the hedge which marked the back perimeter of her property. This seemed to be his appointed time for a daily walk along the path which paralleled the clifftop for at least two miles. Stunning views but only for those with a steady step and a strong head for heights. Erosion had been taking its toll for some years now.

The layout of the four houses in the tiny cul-de-sac, which with a singular lack of imagination had been christened Clifftop Drive, meant that the rear of the properties, just at present, had acquired more importance than their frontage. Since the Local Town Council had begun their annual Spring mauling of the road surface of the Drive, the occupants had been forced to enter their homes from the back lane. The obstacle course at the front - huge holes, Caterpillar diggers, mounds of earth and old tarmac - made it impossible for them to go inside any other way. However, Number Two was used only in the summer months as a holiday home. Number Four was empty, the subject of a protracted inheritance battle since Mr Charles had died there five years earlier. So the only two who were inconvenienced were herself in Number Six, and her new enigmatic neighbour in Number Eight. He'd moved in two months ago. She shook her head as she realised how very little she knew of him.

It wasn't nosiness. Far from it! In her own past she'd suffered too much from the intrusive curiosity of others. She just found it hard to comprehend how you could live next door to someone for two months, and glean so little. Granted, the privet hedges of Number Eight were thick and high, its fences were over six-foot tall, and thus, even from the very bottom of her back garden, she could glimpse only its third floor. Being the last house in the row before the cliff dropped away meant there was no way to see any more of the house from the other side either. A few months ago, while she'd been pruning the Escallonia hedge at the front, she'd chatted with the Estate Agent, an old school friend, while he was waiting to open up and 'show' the house. He gave her the distinct impression that this extreme level of privacy was one of the property's chief attractions for this particular client.

After the house had been bought, the necessary changes by assorted workmen made and her new neighbour installed, she realised this had indeed been a valid observation. Groceries were delivered in a supermarket van once a week. The Pharmacy delivered a prescription once a fortnight. The car parked in the driveway never moved. No-one ever visited. She herself valued a quiet life, especially in recent years, and thus appreciated that the Drive was such a secluded place in which to live, but even for her this level of isolation seemed extreme.

Conscious of at least one potential danger in living alone, she looked out for him each day at 2.15, just to reassure herself that he was still alive. What if during the night he had fallen, lay injured, was perhaps dying. She was unaware of the small daily sigh of relief she gave when she saw him appear. Not that she could see much. He always wore a full-length Australian Outback coat – all enveloping, steel grey, lapels pulled up high around his neck - with a matching Cowboy hat, brim turned down to shield his face. Leather gloves matched the coat. Sturdy boots were worn to provide a firm grip on the stony cliff path. In the beginning she had applauded the look as stylish but as day after day passed, he always wearing the same ensemble, she wondered. She had no idea what he looked like, bar the fact that he was over six-foot, medium of build and walked with athleticism. Why such a need for anonymity?

Mind you, she was only too willing to acknowledge his right to it. She'd had such a hard fight to find it herself in recent years. A lifetime ago - but in reality only eighteen years - she'd been a leading catwalk model. A cream complexion, swathe of thick blonde hair, endless legs, calm patience throughout all the tedious hours of reshooting and restyling, and a skinniness bordering on anorexia made her one of the Darlings of the Fashion Press. When her relationship with playboy millionaire Ramil Abdul became public knowledge, her face featured with regularity on the frontpages of glossy magazines worldwide. She was the perfect foil for his dark Byronic image, he as broody as she was wholesome. She found him irresistible. Even used as she was to the stunning profiles of male models, she thought he was the most beautiful man on the planet. Not just handsome … but beautiful. He knew just how to flick her a sideways glance, arch an eyebrow, or flash a grin of charismatic charm to keep her spell-bound, mesmerized by every nuance of his face.

She never wavered in her adoration – despite his narcissism, sense of entitlement, draining demands on her emotional energy and the regular tabloid reveals about other women. Then came the night of the British Fashion Awards. A new Porsche, a crystal cascade of free champagne, an excess of adoration from the glitterati combined to exhilarate him beyond recklessness. He insisted on driving home. The crash killed him, and lacerated her womb. She left the private hospital a fortnight later. In shock, processing her grief, facing a child-barren future, she fled home to her parents' house on the south coast.

She intended to stay just until she felt healed, but callous Fate was not done with her just yet. A cancerous tumour forced her mother into a spiral of chemo deterioration. As her only child, Izzy stayed to nurse her until her end. The loss was too much for her father. His dementia was savage in the speed of its onset. Izzy stayed to cherish him until his end, albeit in a care home at the last. It was a time beyond measuring before she could raise her eyes, straighten her shoulders, and look at horizons again. With no desire to return to her previous life, nor trial any new one, a comfortable financial inheritance, which included the house, allowed her to sink with relief into the peace and calm of Number Six, Clifftop Drive.

So, while she was willing to look out for her neighbour every day to check he was having his daily walk, she was also respectful of his boundaries. She'd had such a painful journey building her own. This was why she was faced with such a dilemma one Thursday evening. Returning from a visit to a local craft shop, she turned the corner into the back lane to enter her house through the rear garden. There in the evening gloom, leaning against her gate, was a rectangular package, the size of a small suitcase. *Yet another delivery at the back. When will they ever finish those blasted roadworks!* She sighed, dreading the effort required to carry it up the garden path to the kitchen door. In her mind, she scrolled through her recent online orders but came up with nothing that size. It started to drizzle. *Oh Lord, best get it out of the wet!* It wouldn't budge, weighed far too much for her to lift. As she gave it a rather bad-tempered kick, she registered the label. The address read Mr Adam Bett, Number Eight, Clifftop Drive.

Afterwards she said that if she hadn't been so tired and damp, if she hadn't been so angry with the delivery man and the eternal roadworks, if the package hadn't been so heavy, she'd never have done what she did. She marched to the gate next door, started to pound on it. With increasing annoyance as her rational self-suspected he'd never hear her knocking, in spite of feeling that what she was doing was wrong, and with the rain getting heavier, she grabbed the latch, shoving her shoulder against the gate. Not closed with proper care earlier in the afternoon, it swung open. She fell through. Lacking balance she toppled over, landing on the damp paved path in an undignified slither, feeling her ankle twist. *Oh no, this isn't happening. It can't be.*

As she scrabbled to right herself, trying to ignore the stab of burning pain shooting up her calf, from behind she felt two hands slide under her arms, lifting her. She could not have said which was worse - the throbbing in her ankle or the torturous embarrassment flooding her body. She heard herself erupt in a torrent of explanation and apology, trying to explain away her intrusion, the open gate, the lack of dignity in her situation. The hands behind continued to help her up, taking the weight off her leg.

The silence of her rescuer unnerving her even more, her spate of words wound down only when she realized she had been half-carried, half-hoisted to an open kitchen door. Ahead lay a warm picture-book room, complete with an oaken table and chairs, orange Le Creuset accessories hanging from the shelves, many green flowering plants and two large velveteen armchairs in front of an Aga.

Please sit in one of the chairs. I'll get you a towel and some ice for that ankle. All this in a slow American drawl. She sagged in resignation, allowing herself to be propelled forward. Sinking into the closer armchair, she turned to thank her rescuer. *No don't! Don't turn round just yet.* She heard the words too late. She had already turned. She stared, her thanks stifled. To her horror she found she could not look away, could only continue to take in the details. In front of her was a tall, well - built man, early forties she'd guess, dressed in casual denim. His hair was neck length, jet black, silky-sheened, his jaw well defined, his colouring pale. Well-regulated features … on one side of his head. On the other, it seemed as if every surface had melted, had congealed into a dull red atrocity in which no single feature could be defined. Furthermore, a claw-like appendage replaced the hand on that same side.

She hadn't stopped talking from the gate to the chair. Now she felt as if there was nothing she could possibly say. *It's all right, everyone reacts that way.* That was much kinder than she deserved. She was being so crass. In a quiet monotone voice, as he boiled a kettle, prepared cups, made coffee, he continued to speak, to veil the embarrassment of her silence. *I used to be a pilot, working for the Red Cross. My plane crashed. Went up in flames. The surgeons say that more corrective work can be done…but I'm weary of the operations, the hospitals. I prefer now just to tuck myself away … here in England. Thousands of miles away from anyone who knows what I used to be.* The words had an unnatural ring about them, like that of an over-rehearsed speech.

All of a sudden, much to her own surprise, a dam in her burst wide. She heard herself explaining that she understood the need to withdraw from an ungracious world. She told him about Ramil, the accident, the hysterectomy. She described the slow dying of both her parents. She talked of the long nights spent looking into the dark, the free-fall of facing a life without meaning, of fearing the loneliness of an empty future. She strained to convince him that perhaps her inner life mirrored his. As he listened without interruption, he realised he was hearing the truth of her. She did know, she did understand. He yielded…and spoke his truth back to her.

It was only the first night of many such revealings, of many such communications. Over time, the two houses became one building. Izzy and Adam married and adopted. The external pain of the operations became only a memory, the internal pain of isolation an echo in a distant past. Each year on the anniversary of that long ago rainy Thursday, they drank a toast to an unknown delivery man who would never know his contribution to their Happy Ever After.

Footnote:

The main characters are called;

Izzy (Bellamy) & (Adam) Bett

Isabelle (belle âme) & Bett

Belle (beautiful soul) & Bête

Beauty & Beast

Butterflies and Phoenixes

never in a better *Now*
to stand and stare
prioritise   recalibrate
don't look back!
heed Lot's wife
her salty sting of memory

on the cliffs edge
steady   find balance
prepare
appraise
what to jettison
cast off   let go

the Fool on the hill
his world spinning round,
has no fear   he leaps
as we will when our mire
curves dreamward again

slough shells
scrape barnacles
shed weight
pause for just this moment
before celebrating
butterflies and phoenixes.

In this Trilogy of Books

- It's like Walking a Tightrope
- Out of the Chrysalis
- A Phoenix Still Rising

Techniques used:

Micro Poetry	- generally less than 100 words
Flash Fiction	- generally less than 500 words
Shory Stories	
Poetry	
Ekphrastic Writing	- writing inspired by other art, i.e. painting, photography, music
Abecedarian Writing	- a 26-line piece, each beginning alphabetically with A, B, etc.
Dialogue pieces	
Concrete Poetry	- poetry conveyed visually, using patterns of words, fonts, etc.

Formatted Prose pieces

Line/Hook Poetry	- using repeated lines, or hooks such as the senses, as the structural model
Acrostics	- a piece in which letters in each line form a word or words

Speeches by Literary Characters

A series of linked newspaper Article excerpts

About the Author

On returning from S.W. France to live in Northern Ireland, a retired teacher of twenty-six years, Mary Farrell joined her first Creative Writing Group in Flowerfield Arts Centre in Portstewart, Northern Ireland, in 2017. For the last four years a Facilitator of the u3a North Coast Writers Group, she is now in her second year as a member of the Judging Panel for the Weekly Prompts Competition run by the Reedsy Online Publishing Company. For The NI Library Authority, she facilitates Words Inc, the Coleraine Library Creative Writing Group, and also co-ordinates an independent third weekly Writing Group in Portstewart called Sanderlings.

She has been a member of CIEP, The Chartered Institute of Editing and Proofreading, UK, and is the Consultant Creative Writing Facilitator for Impspired Press, based in Lincoln.

Her first Collection of varied pieces, *It's like Walking a Tightrope* was published in September 2021, and her second *Out of the Chrysalis* in May 2022. *Springboards: a Creative Writing Manual for Beginners through to Facilitators,* and *The Kingdom,* her debut Collection of short stories, the first part of *The Circle Trilogy,* were both published in October 2022. She is the Editor of two North Coat Writers Anthologies, *Irish Hares and Seahorses,* 2022, and *Spun Yarns and Woven Words,* 2023, also published by Impspired Press.

She read her own work on BBC Radio Ulster in September 2018 and was a guest on the Time of Our Lives show, also on BBC Radio Ulster, in 2019. Having performed on stage at Tenx9 events in 2018, 2019, 2022 and 2023, also in 2019 she performed at Open Mic Sessions in Portstewart, Northern Ireland. Her short story, *A Tale of a Barn* won the Lurig Drama Club Competition in 2020. Recorded by the actor Ciaran Hinds on November 26th, 2020, it can be found at www.thenineglens.com. She has had various pieces of Prose and Poetry published in Magazines and Anthologies, both locally and internationally.

Printed in Great Britain
by Amazon

21518074R00078